One, two, skip a few,
Ninety-nine, a hundred!

Barefoot Books
2067 Massachusetts Ave
Cambridge, MA, 02140

Grateful acknowledgement is made to the following author and publisher for permission to reprint material copyrighted by them: Puffin Books for 'Four little fishes swimming out to sea' by Glenda Banks, from *This Little Puffin*, compiled by Elizabeth Matterson (1969)

First published in hardcover in the United States of America in 1998 by Barefoot Books, Inc.
First paperback edition printed in 2000.

This book is printed on 100% acid-free paper. Graphic design by Tom Grzelinski, England.
Color reproduction by Columbie Overseas Marketing (Pte) Ltd.
Printed and bound in Singapore by Tien Wah Press (Pte) Ltd.

3 5 7 9 8 6 4

U.S. Cataloging-in-Publication Data / Library of Congress Standards prepared for the hardback edition (1998):

Arenson, Roberta.
One, two, skip a few! : first number rhymes featuring Roberta Arenson.
[32] p. : col. Ill.; 27cm.
Summary: Practice counting skills with old and new rhymes featuring five speckled frogs, three wee monkeys and eight magpies. Jaunty rhymes brought to life by bright and colorful cut-paper collages, ensuring to entrance young children.
ISBN: 1-901223-99X ISBN 1-84148-130-0 (pbk.)
1.Counting-out rhymes. 2. Nursery rhymes. 3. Counting — Poetry.
I. Arenson, Roberta, ill. II. Title.
398.8 —dc21 1998 AC CIP

First Number Rhymes

Illustrated by Roberta Arenson

Barefoot Books
Celebrating Art and Story

One, two, three, four,
Mary at the cottage door;
Five, six, seven, eight,
Eating cherries off a plate.

One potato,
Two potato,
Three potato,
Four;
Five potato,
Six potato,
Seven potato,
More.

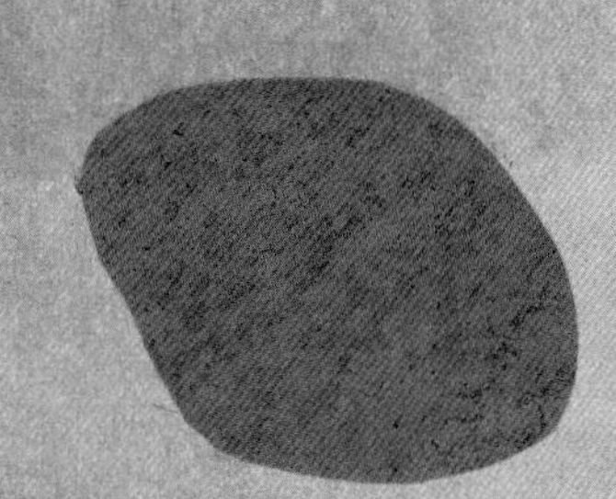

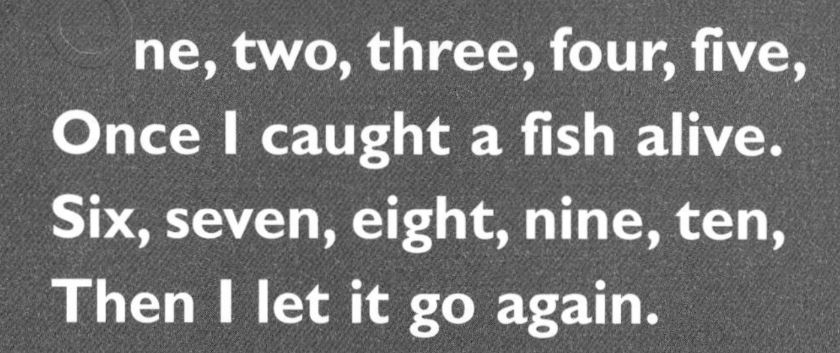

One, two, three, four, five,
Once I caught a fish alive.
Six, seven, eight, nine, ten,
Then I let it go again.

Why did you let it go?
Because it bit my finger so.
Which finger did it bite?
This little finger on my right.

Here is the beehive,
Where are the bees?
Hidden away where nobody sees.
Soon they come creeping, out of the hive,
One! Two! Three! Four! Five!

Five eggs and five eggs, that makes ten.
Sitting on top is a mother hen.
Crackle, crackle, crackle,
What do you see?
Ten yellow chicks, fluffy as can be.

Ha ha ha, hee hee hee,
Three wee monkeys up a tree.
One fell down and hurt his knee,
Ha ha ha, hee hee hee.

One, two, I love you,
Two, three, do you love me?
Three, four, are you sure?
Four, five, long as I'm alive!

Five busy farmers
Woke up with the sun,
For it was early morning
And chores must be done.

The first busy farmer
Went to milk the cow,
The second busy farmer
Thought he'd better plow.

The third busy farmer
Fed the hungry hens,
The fourth busy farmer
Mended broken pens.

The fifth busy farmer
Took his vegetables to town,
Baskets filled with cabbages
And sweet potatoes, brown.

When the work was finished
And the western sky was red,
Five busy farmers
Tumbled into bed.

Said the first little chicken,
With an odd little squirm:
"I wish I could find
A fat little worm!"

Said the second little chicken,
With an odd little shrug:
"I wish I could find
A fat little bug!"

Said the third little chicken,
With a small sigh of grief:
"I wish I could find
A green little leaf!"

Said the fourth little chicken,
With a faint little moan:
"I wish I could find
A wee gravel stone!"

"Now see here!" said the mother,
From the green garden patch:
"If you want any breakfast,
Just come here and scratch!"

Four little fishes swimming out to sea,
One met a shark!
And then there were three.

Three little fishes wondering what to do,
One hid in a great big shell,
And then there were two.

Two little fishes looking for some fun,
One chased after a wave,
And that left only one.

One little fish with all his friends gone,
Went back home to find his mum,
And that left none!

Five rosy apples hanging on a tree,
The rosiest apples you ever did see.
Along came the wind and gave a big blow,
And one rosy apple fell down below.

Four rosy apples hanging on a tree,
(repeat)

I saw eight magpies in a tree,
Two for you and six for me;
One for sorrow, two for mirth,
Three for a wedding, four for a birth;
Five for England, six for France,
Seven for a fiddler, eight for a dance.

One little elephant went out one day,
Upon a spider's web to play;
He had such tremendous fun,
He sent for another elephant to come.

Two little elephants went out one day,
(repeat)

Five little speckled frogs,
Sat on a speckled log,
Eating the most delicious bugs,
"Yum, yum!"
One jumped into the pool,
Where it was nice and cool,
Then there were four green speckled frogs.
"Glub, glub!"

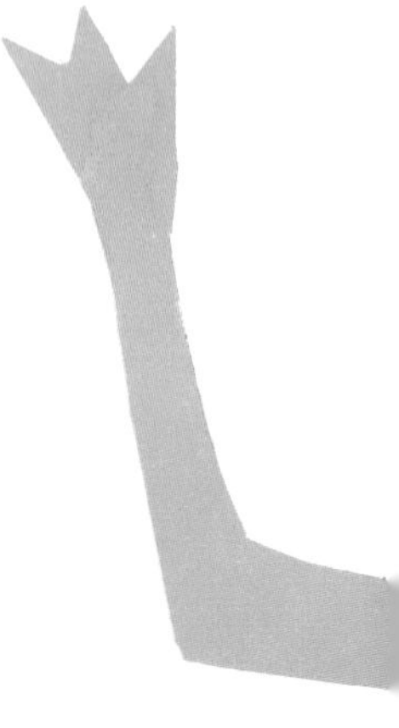

(repeat, until...)

One little speckled frog,
Sat on a speckled log,
Eating the most delicious bugs,
"Yum, yum!"
It jumped into the pool,
Where it was nice and cool,
Then there were no green speckled frogs.
"Glub, glub!"

There were ten in the bed,
And the little one said:
"Roll over, roll over."
So they all rolled over
And one fell out.

There were nine in the bed,
(repeat, until)

There was one in the bed,
And he said:
"Roll over, roll over."
So he rolled over,
And he fell out.

There were none in the bed,
So nobody said:
"Roll over, roll over."

As I was going to St Ives,
I met a man with seven wives,
Each wife had seven sacks,
Each sack had seven cats,
Each cat had seven kits,
Kits, cats, sacks and wives,
How many were going to St Ives?

Twice one are two,
Violets white and blue.

Twice two are four,
Sunflowers at the door.

Twice three are six,
Sweet peas on their sticks.

Twice four are eight,
Poppies at the gate.

Twice five are ten,
Pansies bloom again.

Twice six are twelve,
Pinks for those who delve.

Twice seven are fourteen,
Flowers of the runner bean.

Twice eight are sixteen,
Clinging ivy, evergreen.

Twice nine are eighteen,
Purple thistles to be seen.

Twice ten are twenty,
Hollyhocks in plenty.

Twice eleven are twenty-two,
Daisies wet from morning dew.

Twice twelve are twenty-four,
Roses, who could ask for more?

Eight eights are sixty-four,
Multiply by seven.
When it's done,
Carry one
And take away eleven.
Nine nines are eighty-one,
Multiply by three.
If it's more,
Carry four,
And then it's time for tea!

Go to bed first,
A golden purse.
Go to bed second,
A golden pheasant.
Go to bed third,
A golden bird.

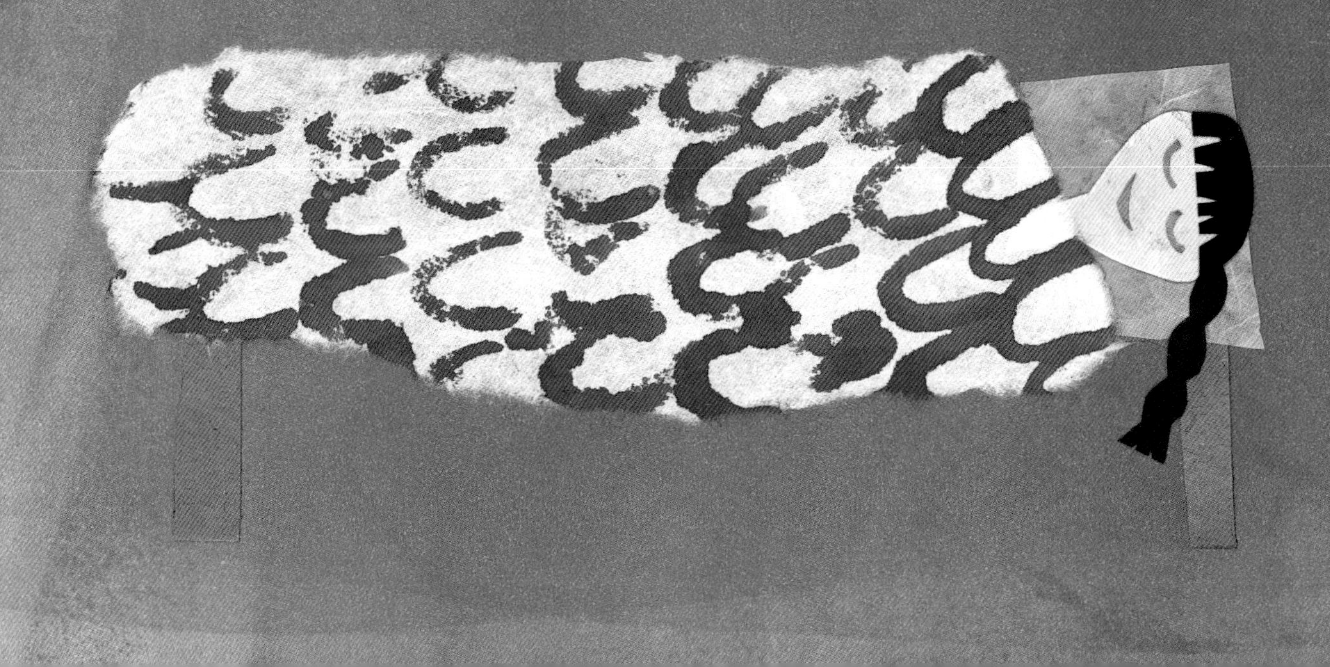

At Barefoot Books, we celebrate art and story with books that open the hearts and minds of children from all walks of life, inspiring them to read deeper, search further, and explore their own creative gifts. Taking our inspiration from many different cultures, we focus on themes that encourage independence of spirit, enthusiasm for learning, and acceptance of other traditions. Thoughtfully prepared by writers, artists, and storytellers from all over the world, our products combine the best of the present with the best of the past to educate our children as the caretakers of tomorrow.

www.barefootbooks.com